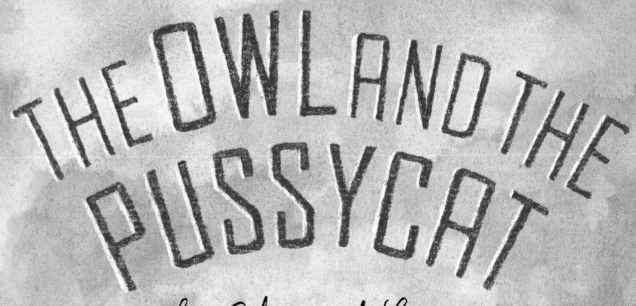

THE OWL AND THE PUSSYCAT

by Edward Lear

Pictures by James Marshall

Afterword by Maurice Sendak

Michael di Capua Books · HarperCollins · Publishers

For William James Gray

In a beautiful pea-green boat.

They took some honey, and plenty of money,
Wrapped up in a five-pound note.

The Owl looked up to the stars above,
And sang to a small guitar,
"O lovely Pussy! O Pussy, my love,
What a beautiful Pussy you are,
    You are,
      You are!
What a beautiful Pussy
    You are!"

Pussy said to the Owl, "You elegant fowl!
How charmingly sweet you sing!
O let us be married! Too long we have tarried—
But what shall we do for a ring?"

They sailed away, for a year and a day,

To the land where the bong tree grows.

And there in a wood a Piggywig stood
With a ring at the end of his nose,
His nose,
His nose,

With a ring at the end of
His nose.

"Dear Pig, are you willing to sell for one shilling Your ring?"

Said the Piggy, "I will."

So they took it away and were married next day

By the Turkey who lives on the hill.

They dined on mince, and slices of quince,
Which they ate with a runcible spoon.

And hand in hand, on the edge of the sand,
They danced by the light of the moon,
The moon,
The moon,

They danced by the light of the moon.

AFTERWORD

James, as usual, prepared the ideal lunch: delectable fresh food (loaded with calories); a light, subtle wine chosen by the proud connoisseur; and a table set brightly, exquisitely. All this despite his very bad health and the slimy summer weather. James Marshall was a perfectionist in all things. And that was precisely the reason for his hesitation about whether to publish his version of *The Owl and the Pussycat*.

With lunch finished, and all cackling gossip exhausted, we settled down to the real purpose of my visit: the careful scrutiny of his working watercolors for the Lear ballad. He knew it was more than likely that he wouldn't live to "finish" this book, in the sense of redoing all the pictures; in his sense, simply, of perfecting them. In my opinion—and I told him so—his professional ethics and very real anxiety had momentarily clouded his judgment. Better than anyone else he knew, I could understand that demanding, sometimes neurotic urge to redo and redo until the sheer punishment of it all convinces us that the work *has* to be finished and is the best we can do. But in this case the problem was easily solved. His pictures for *The Owl and the Pussycat* were perfect.

How could it not be so? With his enormous talent and great courage, James had turned into a shining Prospero in the months before his death, and that magic touch had transformed the ubiquitous ballad into something strangely moving and altogether personal. There was, of course, the trademark Marshall nuttiness that defines James' best work. But this charming slap-happiness was now wed to an odd poignancy that conjured a sweet new essence. This is not to sentimentalize James' last work. Our friendship was too valuable for me to have been anything less than ruthlessly honest with him. I was the older one and had played pal and mentor for well over a decade, and James' present condition absolutely demanded the strictest truth. My enthusiasm was genuine and my wholehearted endorsement for publishing these rich and fabulous "sketches" made him happy.

There were other endorsements from close friends in and out of the publishing world, but I flatter myself that our relationship, both professional and personal, was something unique to both of us. I do not, however, flatter myself into believing that I convinced him to publish these beautiful pictures. He knew—I know he knew—just how rare and wonderful they are. There never was such an Owl and Pussycat, certainly not since Edward Lear, and for my money James surpasses Lear's original pictures in sheer giddy humor and heartfeltness. There never was another such as James Marshall, and my joy at playing a useful role on that summer afternoon toward the end of his life is matched only by my misery at the loss of this brilliant artist, this very best friend.

Maurice Sendak

No Monsters Here

To Melanie Colbert, with gratitude
— Sharon

For Deb, who told me I came from Mars
— Ruth

In Canada
Fitzhenry & Whiteside Limited
195 Allstate Parkway
Markham, Ontario   L3R 4T8

www.fitzhenry.ca

In the United States
Fitzhenry & Whiteside Limited
121 Harvard Avenue, Suite 2
Allston, Massachusetts 02134

godwit@fitzhenry.ca

10 9 8 7 6 5 4 3 2

National Library of Canada Cataloguing in Publication

Jennings, Sharon
     No monsters here / Sharon Jennings ; illustrations by Ruth Ohi.

For children aged 3-6.
ISBN 1-55041-787-8 (bound).—ISBN 1-55041-789-4 (pbk.)

I. Ohi, Ruth II. Title.

PS8569.E563N6 2004   jC813'.54   C2003-907364-5

Publisher Cataloging-in-Publication Data
(Library of Congress Standards)

Jennings, Sharon.
No monsters here / Sharon Jennings ; illustrations by Ruth Ohi.—1st ed.
[24] p. : col. ill. ; cm.
Summary: A brave little boy assures his timid father that there is nothing to fear in this role-reversal story where the monsters are more interested in cookies than giving anyone a real scare.
ISBN 1-55041-787-8
ISBN 1-55041-789-4 (pbk.)
1. Courage – Fiction – Juvenile literature. 2. Fathers and sons – Fiction – Juvenile literature. (1. Courage – Fiction. 2. Fathers and sons – Fiction.) I. Ohi, Ruth. II. Title.
[E] 21   PZ7. J466Nm 2004

Fitzhenry & Whiteside acknowledges with thanks the Canada Council for the Arts, the Government of Canada through its Book Publishing Industry Development Program, and the Ontario Arts Council for their support of our publishing program.

Printed in Hong Kong

Design by Blair Kerrigan/Glyphics

No Monsters Here

Sharon Jennings • Ruth Ohi

Fitzhenry & Whiteside

My father does not want
me to go to bed. He is
afraid of monsters.

Every night, when it starts to
get late, my father looks at the clock.

"I think that clock is broken," he says.
"It isn't time for bed. You can stay up a bit longer."

"But I *want* to go to bed," I tell him. "I am very very tired."

My father takes me to the kitchen. "Would you like another cookie?" he asks.

"I have had enough cookies," I tell him. "I want to go to sleep."

We stand at the bottom
of the stairs. It is dark at the top.
My father sighs a very big sigh.

"I will hold your hand," I tell him.

At my bedroom door, my father asks,
"Wouldn't you like to sleep in my room tonight?"

"No," I say. "I like my own room best."

I turn on my light and look around. "You can come in now," I let my father know.

But he shakes his head. He is afraid of monsters.

"Look under the bed," my father says.

So I do. There's nothing there but toys.

"No monsters here," I tell him.

"Look in the closet," my father says.

So I do. There's nothing there but clothes.

"No monsters here," I tell him.

"Look behind the curtains," my father says.

So I do. There's nothing there but night.

"No monsters here," I tell him.

"Look under the covers," my father says.

So I do. There's nothing there but me.

"I am not a monster," I tell him.

My father takes giant steps to jump on my bed.

"Now we can read a story," I tell him.

"Don't pick a scary one," my father says.

We finish our book.

"Please," my father asks. "Just one more story?"

"No," I tell him. "One story is enough."

I kiss my father and say goodnight. I tell him he can leave the door open just a little bit.

"I'll hear you if you need me in the night," I say.

I listen as my father goes back downstairs.
He is all alone, and he is afraid of monsters.

I am all alone, too.

I go downstairs to find my father.

I sigh a very big sigh.
"Maybe I will have one more cookie," I tell him.

"And I'll read you one more story."